Wild Fa

Lily's Water Woes

Written by Brandi Dougherty
Illustrated by Renée Kurilla

RODALE
KIDS

For my parents, John and Jan
—B.D.

For my sister-in-law Kim, who, like Indigo,
is always dreaming up the most thoughtful surprises!
—R.K.

Copyright © 2018 by Penguin Random House LLC

All rights reserved. Published in the United States by Rodale Kids,
an imprint of Random House Children's Books, a division of Penguin Random House LLC,
New York. Originally published in hardcover in the United States by Rodale Kids,
an imprint of Random House Children's Books, a division of
Penguin Random House LLC, New York, in 2018.

Rodale and the colophon are registered trademarks
and Rodale Kids is a trademark of Penguin Random House LLC.

Visit us on the Web! rhcbooks.com

Educators and librarians, for a variety of teaching tools, visit us at RHTeachersLibrarians.com

Library of Congress Cataloging-in-Publication Data is available upon request.
ISBN 978-1-63565-135-5 (trade) | ISBN 978-1-63565-136-2 (ebook) |
ISBN 978-1-63565-134-8 (pbk.)

MANUFACTURED IN CHINA
10 9 8 7 6 5 4 3 2 1
First Paperback Edition

Contents

Chapter 1

It was a warm spring morning. The wild fairies flitted around the Great Hall of Sugar Oak. Buds of green were popping up all over their beautiful, old oak tree home. The sun danced between the branches. And everybody talked at once.

"I liked the hazelnut stew best," Thistle said. His purple hair stood out sharply, just like his spiky wings.

"Don't forget the honey cakes!" Daisy said. The white petals of her dress swished back and forth as she spoke. "They were *so* yummy!"

They were talking about the Blossom Bash. It was the forest's big festival to celebrate the first bloom of spring. And the wild fairies were the hosts this year. They had been worried about decorating Sugar Oak in time, but thanks to Daisy, it was a huge success and everybody had the best time!

"The entertainment was amazing," said Dahlia. Her squirrel friend, Peanut, bobbed his head in agreement.

"Yes!" Heather nodded. "Celosia's song was so wonderful."

"Thank you," Celosia said and smiled. "But Lily's dance was my absolute favorite."

Lily put her hand to her heart. "Aw, thanks, C! I've already started working on a new water routine." Lily swirled her hands in the air, mimicking her movements through the water. "This one is going to have an even bigger splash finale than the one at Blossom Bash!" Lily told her friends.

"I love it already!" Poppy said.

Just then Lily's frog friend, Splash, croaked. "You're right, Splash. We'd better get back to the pond." Since Lily was a wild fairy *and* a mermaid, she couldn't be away from the water

for very long. "See you tomorrow, everyone."
Lily climbed onto Splash's back, and he hopped
out the door of the Great Hall.

"Bye, Lily! Bye, Splash!" the wild fairies
called.

Chapter 2

The next morning, Lily and Splash played a game at the pond.

"Your turn, Splash!" Lily shouted. Splash pushed out of the pond and blew a huge bubble. Then he nudged it away with his nose. They watched the giant bubble float through the air and then skim across the water toward Lily. She swam toward it and poked the bubble with her finger. It popped right in her face. They laughed.

"Okay, my turn," Lily said, as she started
to blow her own bubble. But Splash hopped up
beside her and got comfortable on a lily pad.
He let out a breath. Lily pushed her elbows
up onto the lily pad and rested her chin in
her hand. "You're bored, aren't you?"

Splash nodded his head. Lily also blew out a breath, making her aqua-blue hair puff away from her face. "I'm bored, too." She looked to the shore. The pebbly beach was empty. In the water sat Lily's cozy cottage. But it was empty, too. None of Lily's friends had come by to visit her today.

"Where is everybody?" she asked.

Splash croaked. "Yeah, maybe you're right," Lily sighed. "They probably stayed up late playing games." Lily wished she could stay late and play games after dinner, too. She always

had to leave first so
she could get back to the pond.

Lily slipped off the pad and dipped into
the water. She did a little twirl and surfaced
again next to Splash. "Come on," she said with
a smile. "Let's find something else to do."

Chapter 3

After lunch, Daisy and Celosia flew down to visit Lily at the pond. Daisy's sidekick, Bumble, and Celosia's sparrow friend, Chirp, joined them. The green buds of spring seemed to be growing bigger by the minute. Soon the tree would be covered in bright-green leaves.

"The sun looks like diamonds on the water!" Celosia pointed toward the pond. "Hey—I should write a song about that!"

"You should!" Daisy smiled at her friend.

Celosia loved to sing and write poetry and songs. "I would love to hear that song. And I bet Lily would, too."

Celosia flapped her wings excitedly. The pile of blond curls on top of her head bobbed in rhythm. "I think I'm going to go work on it right now," she said. "I'll see you later, okay?"

Daisy laughed. Whenever inspiration called, Celosia listened. "Bye!"

"Say hi to Lily for me!" Celosia called back over her shoulder as she flew toward her Sugar Oak nook. Chirp followed along, happy to help with the melody.

"Come on, Bumble," Daisy said. She guided her green leaf wings toward the shore.

Lily and Splash were resting in the shallow water near Lily's cottage.

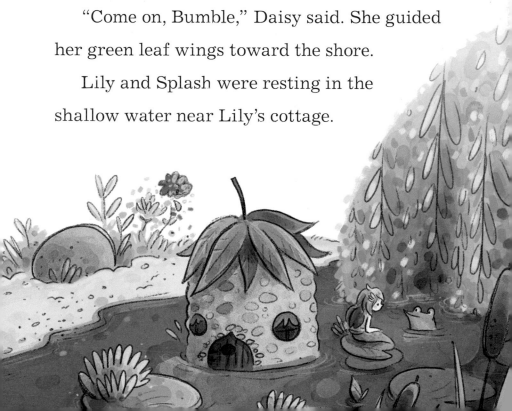

They'd just finished an exhausting game of tag.

"Hi, Lily! Hi, Splash!" Daisy called, settling next to them. She kicked off her shoes and dipped her feet in the water.

"Hey, Daisy," Lily replied, a little breathless.

Daisy held out a small plate for Lily. "I brought you some leftover mushroom pie."

Lily tried to hold back a grimace. She did not like mushroom pie *at all*. "Oh, thanks," she said. "Did I miss lunch again?"

"You did!" Daisy replied. "We watched for you but decided you must be busy."

"Splash and I were just playing tag. I lost track of time!" Lily said.

"I love tag!" Daisy said. "You'll have to let me know next time you play."

Lily nodded. "Are there any *other* leftovers from lunch?"

Daisy shook her head. "I tried to hide the last berry tart under my napkin. But when Dahlia was cleaning up, she thought I'd left it for her as a surprise!" Daisy laughed.

Lily couldn't help but laugh, too. Dahlia loved surprises.

The fairy friends were quiet. Finally, Daisy said, "Celosia says hello!"

"Where is she?" Lily asked. "I wanted to talk to her about my new routine."

"She was going to come with me, but then she got an idea for a song about the pond."

Lily's shoulders slumped. She wanted to know more about Celosia's song. Maybe it would work well with her water dance— especially if it was about the pond.

"I'll tell her to stop by later," Daisy offered.

Lily nodded. But she couldn't help wondering if her friend would really come.

Chapter 4

After Daisy and Bumble said goodbye, Lily and Splash went to Lily's cottage to eat lunch. Splash happily finished the mushroom pie Daisy brought. Lily made herself a seaweed sandwich.

Just then, there was a knock at the door. Poppy peeked her head inside. "Hi! Can we come in?"

Lily smiled. "Sure!"

Poppy, Dahlia, and Thistle squeezed into Lily's tiny cottage. "We wanted to come down and play a game with you!" Thistle said.

"But we didn't mean to interrupt your lunch," Poppy said. "We can come back later . . ."

"That's okay!" Lily said in between mouthfuls of food. A few pieces of her sandwich escaped as she spoke. "I'm a fast eater."

The fairies laughed.

"We just got back from Golden Meadow," Dahlia told Lily. "Peanut wanted to show us all the wildflowers that are blooming."

"I bet they were beautiful," Lily replied. She had always wanted to visit the meadow.

She could only imagine how pretty it must be.

"They were!" Poppy said. Her ladybug sidekick, Spot, buzzed in agreement. "We saw so many shades of red."

"And this evening, we're going to Pine Cone Terrace to watch the sunset with the chipmunks," Thistle said.

"Oh, I wish I could come!" Lily had always been happy with her pond home in the shade of Sugar Oak. But exploring the forest with her friends would be so much fun! She just wished there was a way she could join them . . .

Chapter 5

Later that afternoon, the air began to cool. A breeze skimmed across the pond, making little waves. It would be evening soon. Lily thought about her friends watching the sunset from Pine Cone Terrace. She wondered what it would look like. She loved the sunset she could see from the pond. In fact, it was her favorite thing! But seeing something different— something new—sounded nice, too.

"Hi, hi!" Heather called from the shore, shaking Lily out of her thoughts. Heather's bright-pink, wavy hair swished around her shoulders in the breeze. Flutter hung in the air nearby, and Indigo stood next to her. She had a

small tool belt around the waist of her purple petal dress. Indigo was great at making things.

Lily waved and then swam to the edge of the pond where her friends stood. "What are you working on, Indigo?" she asked.

Indigo's eyes were bright behind the blue and purple streak in her dark hair. "I just started a couple of new projects this morning. I was inspired by Blossom Bash!"

"What are they?" Lily asked. She always liked to hear what Indigo was doing.

"They're kind of hard to explain. You'll just have to see them!"

Lily's mouth turned into a small frown. She realized she hadn't been to Indigo's workshop in ages. It was all the way at the top of Sugar

Oak, so Lily could never stay long before she needed to get back to the pond.

"I brought you some honeysuckle tea!" Heather said. "I know it's your favorite."

Lily smiled, but it wasn't her usual smile— the kind that took up her whole face.

"I loved hearing about your new dance routine last night, Lily!" Indigo said. "I can't wait to see it."

"It still needs work," Lily said, but her voice was so quiet her friends barely heard her. Heather and Indigo exchanged a concerned look.

"Is everything okay, Lily?" Heather asked.

Lily sighed. "I just . . ." She didn't know how to explain it. Besides, she didn't think her friends would understand. "It's nothing," she said. "I'm fine." But she wasn't.

Chapter 6

That night, the wild fairies were cleaning up the Great Hall after dinner. Everyone was there, except for Lily. She and Splash were already back at the pond.

"I'm worried about Lily," Daisy told her friends. "She just doesn't seem like herself today."

The other fairies agreed.

"When Indigo and I visited her before dinner, she was really quiet," Heather told the group.

"She was quiet when we saw her, too," Thistle said. "Especially when we talked about visiting Golden Meadow and Pine Cone Terrace."

"I think she's feeling left out," Daisy said.

"Fiddlesticks!" said Poppy. "I was afraid of that."

"What can we do?" Celosia asked. "She always needs to be near the water."

"Yeah," Heather chimed in. "It's not like she can bring the water with her . . ."

The wild fairies were quiet as they tried to think of a way to help Lily. Indigo thought so hard she spilled a glass of water onto her lap and then slid right out of her chair! Her caterpillar friend, Fuzz, licked the side of her face. Everybody laughed. Then Indigo's eyes got extra big. "I have an idea!" she cried.

Chapter 7

The wild fairies and their animal friends all worked together to bring Indigo's idea to life. They got up early the next morning to start on the plans. They wanted it to be a surprise, so they couldn't show Lily until they were finished. It was hard to keep a secret from their friend, but they knew she would be so happy when she saw what they had done.

It was especially hard for Dahlia to stay quiet. She loved surprises, but she had a hard time with secrets! "Ooooo. I just can't wait!"

she said. Her bright-red pigtails bounced up and down.

Thistle laughed. "I think you better stay away from Lily until we're done!"

Dahlia giggled. "I think you're right. I don't want to ruin it!"

Indigo asked for Poppy's help overseeing the project. Poppy loved to plan things, so she used her clipboard and a pencil to make a chart. She wrote everyone's jobs on her paper and kept track of their progress. Spot helped. Poppy loved it!

"This is going to be great!" Daisy said with a bright smile.

"She's going to love it!" Celosia agreed.

Meanwhile, at the pond, Lily bobbed in the shallow water. She was busy weaving a basket out of reeds. "This is perfect for Indigo to keep her tools in!" she told Splash. "And then I'll make a folder for Celosia to keep her poetry in."

Splash croaked.

"Hey! You're right," Lily replied. "Celosia *is* late. She was supposed to be here to help me with my new water dance routine." Lily frowned. The shore was just as empty as yesterday. In fact, none of her wild fairy friends had been down to the pond all day!

Chapter 8

*L*ily turned to Splash. "Do you think they stayed up late again?" Splash looked up at Sugar Oak. His face perked up. One of the fairies was coming!

Lily smiled, too. It was Celosia. Lily knew she wouldn't forget! Celosia flew fast and skidded to a stop at the edge of the water. Just then, Chirp joined her.

Chirp held a long piece of meadow grass in her beak. Celosia began to pull lily pads out of the water and stack them on Chirp's back. "Hi, Lily!" she called as she worked.

Lily hid the folder she was making for Celosia. "What are you doing?" she asked.

"Oh, I just . . . I'm, uh, helping Indigo with something," Celosia said. She was out of breath from flying fast, and now she

worked quickly at
the edge of the pond.
Lily crinkled her forehead.
Celosia was acting weird! "Are you
ready to help me with my new routine?"
Celosia dropped the lily pad in her hand.

"Oh, Lily! I'm sorry. I forgot!"

"That's okay," Lily said and shrugged. "We can do it now."

The freckles on Celosia's nose twitched. "I can't right now. I have to get these lily pads to Indigo. But later—I promise!" And with that, Celosia tied the piece of grass around Chirp's middle. The two of them flew back to Sugar Oak without another word.

Lily turned to Splash and frowned. "My friends are so busy," she said. "Too busy for me . . ."

Splash hopped up next to Lily and nudged her side. "It's okay," Lily said. "We have each other, right?"

Splash croaked in agreement. But Lily looked toward the shore again.

Chapter 9

The next morning, Lily woke up early and dove into the pond. When she came up, Splash was waiting for her on a lily pad. He held a bunch of pretty wildflowers in his mouth. Lily could see a flower representing each of her wild fairy friends. And right in the middle of the bouquet was a big, blue lily!

"For me?" Lily asked. The frog croaked.
"Thank you, Splash!" Lily took the flowers
and wove them together to make a crown.
She put it on her head and twirled in a circle,
making little ripples in the water. "I'll wear it
all day!"

Lily searched the shore for her friends. But,
just like the day before, it was empty. "Come
on," Lily said to Splash. "Let's have breakfast!"

After breakfast, Splash watched Lily
practice her water routine. When she stopped
to rest, she glanced up at Sugar Oak. It was
quiet. "Everybody's been so busy. Do you
think they forgot about me?" she whispered,
tears filling her eyes.

Splash made a gentle croaking sound. Lily

wiped her eyes. "You're right," she told him. "I can't be sad on such a beautiful day! Hey—let's have an adventure! We can explore the other side of the pond."

Splash immediately hopped into the water. Lily laughed. "Let's go!"

The wild fairies worked hard all morning to finish Lily's surprise. Finally, late that afternoon, they were ready for the big reveal.

"I'm going to sing her my new song about the pond, too," Celosia said as they all flitted down to the water.

"I know she's excited to hear it!" Daisy said.

Dahlia made a funny squeaking sound. "I just can't wait to see her face!"

The fairies laughed.

But when they got down to the shore, it was empty. Poppy looked inside Lily's cottage. "It doesn't look like Lily has been here for a while," she said.

Daisy searched the reeds. Thistle and Spike

flew low over the water to see if Lily was diving underneath. But they only saw three fish and a turtle. Peanut and Chirp called to Splash. There was no answer.

"Where is she?" Poppy asked. She was worried. They all were. Lily was always right here in the pond. She had never gone missing before!

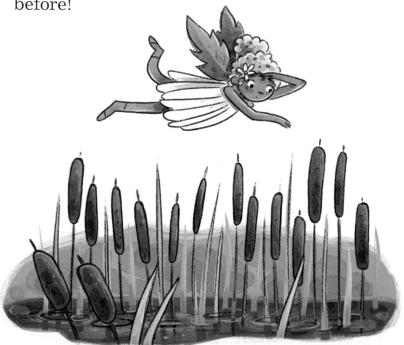

Chapter 10

Daisy held up her hands. "Okay, everybody!" she said in as calm a voice as she could. "Let's split up and look for her."

"Good idea," said Dahlia. "She has to be somewhere near the pond. We'll find her. Don't worry!" The other fairies followed her lead and took a few deep breaths.

Thistle and Spike
stayed near Lily's
cottage in case she
came back. Indigo and

Fuzz, Poppy and Spot took the little wooden
boat and began to row across the pond to
see if Lily was swimming under the water.
Dahlia hopped on Peanut's back to search the
shallow water near the shore. Celosia rode
Chirp high in the sky
to get a view of the
whole pond.

And Daisy and
Bumble, Heather
and Flutter flew

low over the water to look around the lily pads and reeds.

The wild fairy friends searched and searched, calling Lily's name as they looked. The sun began to dip low behind the trees on the other side of the pond. It was getting late. And it was hard not to worry!

"Fiddlesticks!" Poppy cried as she and Indigo reached the other side of the pond. "Where is she?"

Indigo sighed and scanned the shore. Dahlia and Peanut came out of the bushes. Dahlia shook her head.

Just then, bubbles broke on the surface of the pond. "Wait a minute!" Poppy shouted as she pointed to the water. Lily pushed out of the pond with a dramatic twirl. Splash popped out next to her and scrambled onto a lily pad.

"Lily!" all of the wild fairies cried at once.

Lily jumped. She wasn't expecting to see her friends there. "What are you doing here?" she asked.

"Looking for you!" Dahlia said. "We've been searching everywhere."

"You scared us!" Poppy added.

Lily swished her hand through the water. "I decided to

have an adventure today," she said quietly. "I

thought you had forgotten about me . . ."

"We didn't forget about you, Lily." Indigo

reached out of the boat and

squeezed Lily's shoulder.

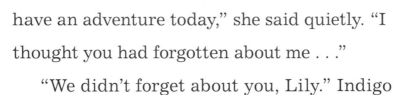

"We've been working on a surprise for you!"

Daisy, Heather, and Celosia fluttered
to a stop above the other fairies. "Come
back home, Lily. It's time to show you your
surprise!" Daisy said.

Lily smiled a big smile. Her friends hadn't
forgotten her. "I'll race you!" she shouted,
before flipping back into the water and
swimming fast toward home.

Chapter 11

When the fairies reached the shore, Chirp, Thistle, and Indigo hurried to unveil the surprise. The fairies had woven lily pads together with thick grass from the meadow. The lily pads created a sturdy basket that they filled with water. The basket had a strong handle made of braided vines. That way, with Chirp's help, Lily could be carried in her basket to places like Golden Meadow and Pine Cone Terrace! Lily could hardly believe her eyes.

"That's not even the best part of the surprise!" Dahlia said. "Come and see!"

Lily followed the other wild fairies to the base of Sugar Oak. Extending up the back of the trunk was a wooden waterslide! The slide went all the way up to Indigo's workshop at the top of the tree.

"Now you can travel up and down Sugar Oak in the water," Daisy said. "Splash can help you!"

Lily gasped. "This is amazing!"

"You won't have to leave early after dinner anymore," Thistle said.

"I can stay and play games!" Lily cried.

"And when you're ready to go back to the pond, you can slide all the way down to the shore!" Heather squeaked.

Lily's eyes filled with tears for
the second time that day. But this time, they
were happy tears.

"I'm sorry you thought we forgot about you,
Lily," Celosia said. "We never wanted you to
feel left out!"

"And I'm sorry that I ever doubted my
friends," Lily said. "You guys are the best!"

The wild fairies huddled into a big group
hug. "So, were you surprised?" Dahlia asked.
"Was I ever!" Lily beamed.

Chapter 12

That evening, Celosia sang her new song about the pond while Lily performed the routine she'd been working on. Lily swam gracefully through the pond. Her arms made perfect circles above her head as she twirled her body and skimmed her tail fin across the top of the water. At the end, she dove deep into the pond and then surfaced with a gentle splash. Everybody clapped and cheered. Lily grinned before taking a bow. She loved performing for her friends.

Then, the wild fairies made their way to the
Great Hall. With Splash's help, Lily happily
made her way up the tree. For dinner, the
fairies ate dandelion salad and fig pies and
drank yummy pomegranate juice. Dahlia told
a funny story about a mix-up with a turtle
on Seashell Beach. Everybody laughed. Lily
couldn't believe that now there was a way
for her to visit Seashell Beach. She'd always
wanted to go!

The wild fairies ended the night with a
game of charades—Lily's favorite. Lily had
more fun than she'd even had at Blossom Bash!
As she and Splash took their new waterslide
back to the pond, Lily couldn't stop smiling.

Her Sugar Oak home had just become that much sweeter—and her friends that much closer.

All About Water Lilies

Water lilies are flowering plants that grow in the soil under the water. They have long, strong stems that push up through the water so that their leaves can rest on the surface. These leaves are called lily pads! The leaves of water lilies are round with a little notch cut out of one side. The notch helps water drain off the leaf so that it can stay afloat. Water lilies grow in still bodies of water like ponds and lakes.

There are different types of water lilies that grow different colors of flowers. Some are white, some are yellow, others are pink. They are all beautiful!

Frogs like to rest on lily pads when they aren't swimming or looking for bugs to eat. They just have to make sure that they aren't too heavy for the lily pad to hold them! Frogs like to relax in the sun but only for a little while. Just like Lily, frogs need to be near water at all times. Otherwise their skin gets too dry. Have you ever seen a frog on a lily pad?

Lily's Friendship Flower Crown

Create your own beautiful flower crown like the one Splash made for his best pal, Lily.

Using just a few household items, you'll be performance ready, just like Lily and Splash!

Cupcake liners, various colors and sizes

Pipe cleaners

Scissors

A pencil

Decorative ribbon, optional

1. Fold a cupcake liner inside out so that the color is on the inside.

2. Fold the liner in half, and then in half again, and then in half again!

3. Cut around the top of the folded liner—you can cut in waves, in points . . . get creative!

4. Unfold, and you have a beautiful flower!

5. Repeat steps 1 through 3 using cupcake liners in different colors and sizes. Don't be afraid to adjust the number of folds and/or the way you cut the liners to see what kind of flower you can create!

6. Once you're happy with all of your flowers, use a pencil to poke a hole through the center of each one, and then string them onto a pipe cleaner with the colorful side facing out.

7. Adjust the pipe cleaner to fit your head, and then twist the two ends of the pipe cleaners together.

You can also cut a piece of pretty ribbon and twist it onto the back of the crown so it hangs down your hair like a long mermaid tail!

What Type of Fairy Are You?

Which of the wild fairy friends are you most like? Answer the following questions and then tally up your answers to find out!

1. Which activity sounds the most fun to you?
   - A. Planning and organizing an event
   - B. Making something new
   - C. Gardening
   - D. Putting on a performance or a show

2. You're getting ready to go to a party. Choose a must-have fairy accessory:
   - A. Wings
   - B. A tool belt
   - C. A tasty snack
   - D. A flower crown

3. What word best describes your personality?
   - A. Determined
   - B. Friendly
   - C. Curious
   - D. Energetic

4. Which school subject would you choose first?
   - A. English
   - B. Math
   - C. Gym
   - D. Choir

5. The wild fairies love the seasons! What's your favorite season?
   - A. Summer
   - B. Winter
   - C. Fall
   - D. Spring

6. Which of these color combinations do
   you like the best?
   A. Green and red
   B. Purple and gray
   C. Pink and orange
   D. Yellow and blue

7. It's a warm summer day. Which wild fairy
   activity do you want to join?
   A. Playing tag
   B. Visiting the bugs in Golden Meadow
   C. Exploring a hidden cave
   D. Swimming in the pond

8. Who's your favorite critter companion?
   A. Bumble
   B. Spike
   C. Peanut
   D. Splash

9. Phew, answering all these questions is making you hungry.
   Which fairy food do you choose to refuel?
   A. Honey cakes
   B. Hazelnut stew
   C. Fresh fruit
   D. Pomegranate puffs

10. Which rainy day activity interests you most?
    A. Chatting with a friend
    B. Scrapbooking
    C. Baking cookies
    D. Writing a story

Mostly As:

If your answers were mostly As, you're
similar to Daisy and Poppy! You like to
plan fun events, and you're very organized
in your day-to-day life. Maybe you make
lists like Poppy does. Or maybe friends
look to you to be the leader in some situations.
You might have a tendency to get worried like Poppy, or
you could be upbeat and positive like Daisy. Either way, you're
a great friend and tons of fun!

Mostly Bs:

Did you choose mostly B responses? Then you're like Thistle and
Indigo! You're crafty and have fun coming up with your own
projects to make. You also love to take care of your friends and
make sure everyone is happy. Maybe you're a bit of a storyteller
like Thistle, or maybe you enjoy helping solve difficult problems
like Indigo. Whatever you do, your friends love having you by
their sides!

Mostly Cs:

If you came up with mostly Cs, then you match up to Heather and
Dahlia! You like to explore and be adventurous. You're curious
and positive and don't get rattled easily. Maybe you love to bake or
experiment in the kitchen as Heather does. Or maybe you can't wait
to go to new places like Dahlia. Whatever your hobbies, friends can
count on you for excitement!

Mostly Ds:
Were your answers mostly Ds? Looks like you're similar to Lily and Celosia! You love to perform—whether it's singing, dancing, playing an instrument, or something else. You adore having an audience to show off your creative talents. Maybe you're a writer like Celosia, or maybe you enjoy being athletic and playful as Lily does. Chances are, friends look to you for having fun!

If your answers ranged from A through D and everywhere in between, don't worry! It just means you have a little bit of each wild fairy's magic inside.

Meet the Wild Fairies!

Get to know the wild fairies
and their critter companions a little
bit better! Read on to find out
more about each friend.

Daisy

Daisy is a natural leader, and she's lots of fun to be around. She has a bubbly personality and a great laugh. The other wild fairies often look to Daisy to guide them through tricky situations.

Likes: Big dinners in the Great Hall with all her friends
Dislikes: Getting dirty
Favorite activity: Party planning
Favorite food: Honey cakes (yum!)
Favorite color: Green
Favorite season: All of them!

Fun fact: Even though Daisy doesn't like to get dirty, she is such a good friend that she once dug in the mud to help Indigo look for a tool she had dropped!

Bumble

Bumble the bumblebee is Daisy's sweet sidekick. Bumble is a great listener and is there for Daisy whenever she needs him.

Poppy

Poppy is a planner! She likes to organize everything to make sure it's just right. But that also means Poppy can be a little stressed out sometimes.

Likes: Making lists
Dislikes: Change
Favorite activity: Playing hide-and-seek or tag
Favorite food: Strawberries
Favorite color: Red, of course!
Favorite season: Summer

Fun fact: Whenever Poppy gets worried about something, she says, "Fiddlesticks!"

Spot

Poppy's friend Spot is a ladybug with bright red wings. She tries very hard to keep Poppy's worry in check and is always there to make her feel calm and happy.

Thistle

Despite his spiky hair and wings, Thistle is very warm and friendly. He's always looking out for others and likes to stay close to his friends in case they need help.

Likes: Telling stories in the Great Hall
Dislikes: Having allergies
Favorite activity: Visiting Pine Cone Terrace
Favorite food: Hazelnut stew
Favorite color: Gray
Favorite season: Winter (there's no pollen in winter!)

Fun fact: Thistle once rescued a baby chipmunk from a pesky raccoon. The chipmunk's family still invites Thistle to dinner!

Spike

Thistle and Spike the beetle go everywhere together. The wild fairies can always count on them for a good story. Spike likes to be silly and makes a great comedy team with Thistle!

Dahlia

Dahlia has an adventurous spirit.
She likes to try new things and
doesn't get worried about much—
she knows things will work out!

Likes: Surprises!
Dislikes: When a friend is sad or upset
Favorite activity: Exploring new places
Favorite food: Apples
Favorite color: Orange
Favorite season: Fall

Fun fact: Dahlia loves surprises, but she's terrible at
keeping secrets! She accidentally spilled the beans
about Thistle's surprise birthday party.

Peanut

Peanut is a red squirrel, and he's just
as adventurous as Dahlia. Peanut is a
big help carrying supplies or pulling
a wagon for building projects.

Heather

Heather's heart is as big as her bright pink hair. She's an amazing cook, and she's also great at coming up with herbal remedies when a fairy feels sick.

Likes: Taking care of her fairy friends
Dislikes: Running low on supplies
Favorite activity: Baking
Favorite food: It's too hard to pick just one!
Favorite color: Pink
Favorite season: Fall

Fun fact: Heather is so in tune with nature that she can sniff out hidden herbs and flowers with her nose!

Flutter

Flutter is a beautiful pink butterfly. She's a whiz at helping Heather in the kitchen. She picks up herbs and spices and drops them in the pot for Heather while she's cooking! Much like Heather's nose, Flutter's antennae are great at finding hidden treats!

Indigo

Indigo is fearless and creative. She spends equal amounts of time creating things in her workshop and exploring the forest. The other wild fairies come to Indigo when they need help solving a problem. She has a unique way of looking at things.

Likes: Challenges!
Dislikes: Being told "no!"
Favorite activity: Inventing things
Favorite food: Fig jam tarts
Favorite color: Purple
Favorite season: Winter

Fun fact: When Indigo injured her wing, she made a glider to help her sail down Sugar Oak to the pond!

Fuzz

Fuzz the caterpillar is a handy helper in Indigo's workshop with lots of hands for holding tools! Fuzz is pretty quiet, but he is sure to let Indigo know when he likes one of her new ideas.

Celosia

Celosia is a talented poet and musician. She has a bright smile and a beautiful voice. She loves to use her music to make her friends happy.

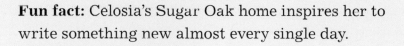

Likes: Writing poems and songs
Dislikes: Gray, dreary weather
Favorite activity: Singing!
Favorite food: Pomegranate puffs
Favorite color: Yellow
Favorite season: Spring

Fun fact: Celosia's Sugar Oak home inspires her to write something new almost every single day.

Chirp

Chirp the sparrow is the perfect companion for a singer like Celosia. Chirp has a lovely singing voice of her own and is happy to provide backup vocals for all of Celosia's songs.

Lily

Lily is a mermaid wild fairy who likes to make a splash! She can be very dramatic and loves to show off a new water dance routine.

Likes: Water ballet
Dislikes: Feeling bored
Favorite activity: Performing
Favorite food: Kelp cupcakes
Favorite color: Blue
Favorite season: Spring

Fun fact: Lily has worked hard to perfect a very difficult stunt. She can now launch herself out of the water and twirl in a perfect circle!

Splash

Splash is a frog and Lily's best friend. They have hours of fun together—from playing games in the pond to eating lunch together in Lily's cozy cottage.

Meet the Author

BRANDI DOUGHERTY is the author of the *New York Times* bestselling picture book *The Littlest Pilgrim* along with six other Littlest tales. She's also written three middle-grade novels, a Pixar picture book, and four books in Giada De Laurentiis's Recipe for Adventure series. She lives in Los Angeles, where she wrangles two adorable kids and one crazy dog with her husband, Joe. Visit brandidougherty.com.

Meet the Illustrator

RENÉE KURILLA has illustrated many books for kids, including *Orangutanka* by Margarita Engle and *The Pickwicks' Picnic* by Carol Brendler. She lives in the woods just south of Boston—the perfect place to search for wild fairies! Visit kurillastration.com.